A Fort on the Moon

Maggie Pouncey

Pictures by Larry Day

NEAL PORTER BOOKS

HOLIDAY HOUSE / NEW YORK

For Felix and Dominic—my favorite explorers,
my imagination teachers, my whole full heart —M.P.

For Andrew and Peter —L.D.

Neal Porter Books

Text copyright © 2020 by Maggie Pouncey
Pictures copyright © 2020 by Larry Day
All Rights Reserved
HOLIDAY HOUSE is registered in the U.S. Patent and Trademark Office.
Printed and bound in June 2020 by Toppan Leefung, DongGuan City, China.
The artwork for this book was created with pencil, pen,
and ink with watercolor and gouache on watercolor paper.
Book design by Jennifer Browne
www.holidayhouse.com
First Edition
1   3   5   7   9   10   8   6   4   2

Library of Congress Cataloging-in-Publication Data

Names: Pouncey, Maggie, author. | Day, Larry, 1956– illustrator.
Title: A fort on the Moon / by Maggie Pouncey ; illustrated by Larry Day.
Description: New York City : Holiday House, 2020. | "Neal Porter Books." |
Audience: Ages 4–8 | Audience: Grades K–1 | Summary: Fox and his younger
brother plan to travel to the moon in a homemade rocket and build a fort.
Identifiers: LCCN 2019039711 | ISBN 9780823446575 (hardcover)
Subjects: CYAC: Imagination—Fiction. | Brothers—Fiction. | Moon—Fiction.
Classification: LCC PZ7.1.P678 Fo 2020 | DDC [E]—dc23
LC record available at https://lccn.loc.gov/2019039711

My big brother Fox Wilder
knows everything about the moon.
Sometimes we go there in a spaceship
we made with odds and ends we
found around the house. We call it
The White Dolphin.

We are preparing for a new voyage.
We build models with our wooden
blocks. We knock them down,
and build them again, better.

"What's all this?" our mother asks us.

So we tell her the truth: "We are building a fort on the moon."

She gets that look grown-ups get when they think you're being cute.

Fox sparkles his green eyes at me, then flashes his dimple at Mama.

Our dad is an engineer, so he thinks he knows
a lot about building.
"How about this?" he asks, moving a key support beam.

"I'm afraid that just won't work," says Fox.

"Did you know," Dad says, "on the moon
there are Peaks of Eternal Light, places
where the sun never sets?"

Did we know? "We've been there
three times," I say.

"Well, four," says Fox.
"If you count the first time."

"Adventurers must be as patient as they are brave!" Fox likes to say.

So we wait. And at last the right night arrives. We lie in our beds, as still as moon craters, till we no longer hear our parents' soft voices and the ribbon of light beneath our door disappears into darkness.

Up, up we go, Fox first, then me, up the corkscrew stairs to the very top of the house. Widow's walk it was called, back when sailors—brave explorers of the sea— lived in this house.

The giant full moon beams down on us like a
lighthouse in the sky.

Our ship, *The White Dolphin*, stands proudly
where we left it, hidden behind the chimney.

We load our materials into the ship, things Mama called junk! Things she'd put in a heap by the back door to be carted away! We bring along, too, our usual tools—Fox's ribbons and my tape collection, two diggers, and two whackers.

Tonight, like Neil Armstrong and Buzz Aldrin, we will land in the Sea of Tranquility. We will build our fort, a home on the moon for all brave enough to use.

Into *The White Dolphin* we climb, helmets clicked, snowsuits zipped. It is cold on the moon. We strap ourselves into our old car seats and Fox counts the numbers down from ten.

"Blast off!" we shout as one.

When you travel to the moon,
you must go very fast, faster than
you've ever gone. The Earth, far
behind you, looks like a marble.

Luckily, the journey is short, when your ship is as good as *The White Dolphin*. We land with a crash, and scrapes and bangs of diggers and whackers. We unclip our harnesses and inspect each other's helmets. We tie ourselves together and to our ship with Fox's ribbons, using the best knots we know—two sailor's fists and a mighty mermaid.

Up close the moon does not glow silver or white or even yellow. Up close it is mysterious and dark, like a mountain turned inside out, a volcano floating in midair. Walking is like walking on the sand of the Earth's softest beach, or stirring the batter of the world's biggest cake.

Things are lighter on the moon. Fox does kangaroo hops, just like Buzz Aldrin. I pick him up and swing him around and it's hilarious. I could never do that back on Earth.

Then it's time to build. But it isn't easy.
In fact, it's harder than we'd imagined.

The moon soil is slippery and our supplies keep tipping
over. Moondust sticks to everything. We're low on tape.

I start to cry, but only a very little.
I want to go home. I hate the moon!

I throw my whacker into the air and
we watch it float away like a lost balloon.

"Adventurers must be as patient as they are brave!" Fox yells.
"And explorers never give up! Not when they've come this far!"
He starts doing some crazy dance moves.

He challenges me to a somersault competition.
We make moon angels.

Then we start to build.
We scoop and tie, stack and lean,
pitch and whack.
We stand back.

It's even better than our models. Dad would be proud of our engineering.

For a moment, we stand inside our hard work and feel proud together.

But adventurers don't stand around applauding themselves! Explorers complete their missions!

We dust each other off, and step back into *The White Dolphin*.

I watch the moon grow smaller and smaller, as Fox watches the Earth grow bigger and bigger. I feel both big and small, brave and scared, patient and restless, so tired and completely awake.

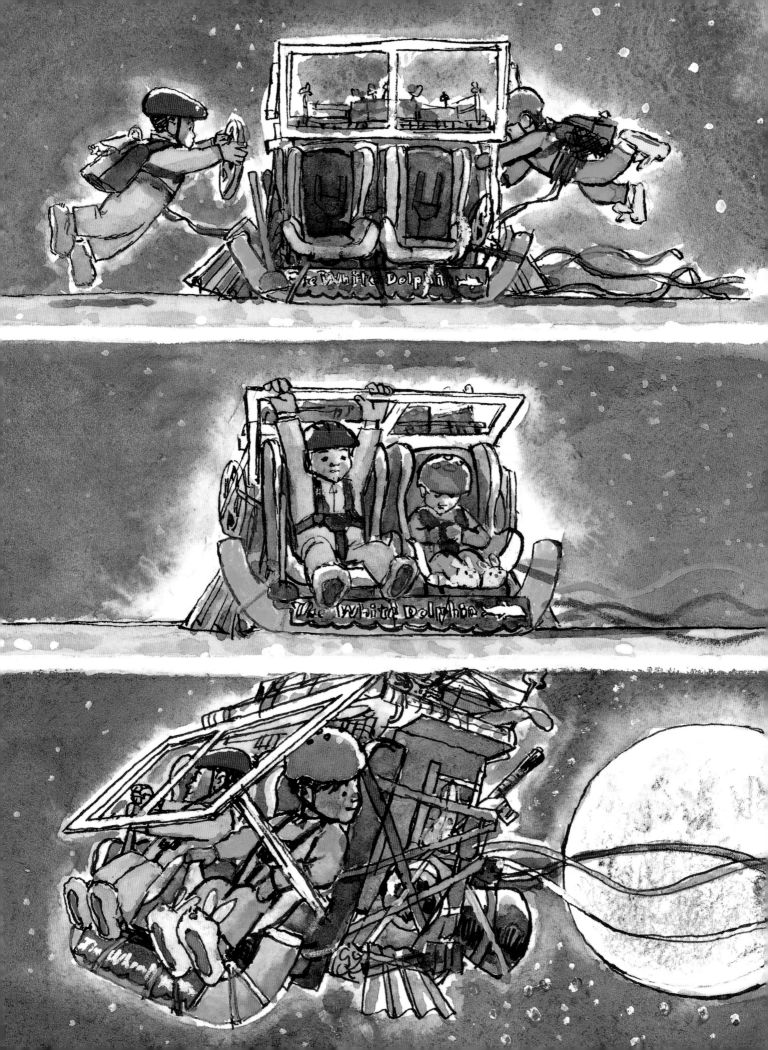

Spotting our widow's walk, Fox
pulls the parachute and we land
on the roof with a soft thud.

He looks at me. "We did it, Dodge."

"I almost didn't," I say. "I wanted to give up."

Fox sits there looking wise. He knows a lot about lots of things, not just the moon. "But you did it anyway," he says.

It is hard to park a spaceship
when you're sleepy.

We pull *The White Dolphin* back
into its hiding spot, behind the
chimney. It will need a good
cleaning and a few repairs
before the next landing.

Soon the sun will rise,
and the moon will disappear
into the pale blue sky of
day. As we climb back into
our house, I turn and
wave goodbye.

In the morning, we eat pancakes shaped like astronauts, stars, and the moon.

"For our brave space explorers," says
our father, as he passes the syrup.

"Has anyone seen that pile of old junk?"
our mother asks. "It's the strangest
thing. Where on Earth could
it have gone?"

In the bright sunlight, Fox's green eyes sparkle, and his dimple flashes. "Outer space?" he says, and I almost fall out of my chair, but our parents just beam at us and dig into breakfast.